EAGLE CREEK PARK

INDIANAPOLIS MOTOR SPEEDWAY MUSEUM

SPEEDWAY INDOOR KARTING

N
W
E
S

For my brother, Don—
the best darn math teacher ever.
Lucky kids. Lucky you.
—Barb

For my Hoosier family and friends: my parents, Louise and Ron Graef of Indianapolis;
my sisters, Rhonda and Holly Graef of Lafayette; the Laughner family;
and my classmates of Taylor High School (outside of Kokomo, Indiana).
—Renée

Barbara, Renée, and Sleeping Bear Press wish to thank the following organizations and businesses
for their assistance: Visit Indianapolis; the Indianapolis Motor Speedway Museum; the Eiteljorg Museum
of American Indians and Western Art; the Children's Museum of Indianapolis; and Newfields.

Library of Congress Cataloging-in-Publication Data
Names: Joosse, Barbara M., author. | Graef, Renée, illustrator. | Title: Lulu & Rocky in Indianapolis | written by Barbara Joosse ; | illustrated by Renée Graef. | Other titles: Lulu and Rocky in
Indianapolis | Description: Ann Arbor, Michigan : Sleeping Bear Press, [2020] | Series: Our city adventures; book 4 | Audience: Ages 4–8 | Summary: "Fox kits Lulu and her cousin Rocky visit
Indianapolis, exploring sights like the Dinosphere at the Children's Museum, Central Canal, Indianapolis Motor Speedway, as well as unexpected gems"– Provided by publisher.
Identifiers: LCCN 2020006323 | ISBN 9781534110663 (hardcover) | Subjects: LCSH: Indianapolis (Ind.)–Description and travel–Juvenile literature. |Classification: LCC F534.I3 J66 2020 |
DDC 917.72/5204–dc23 |LC record available at https://lccn.loc.gov/2020006323

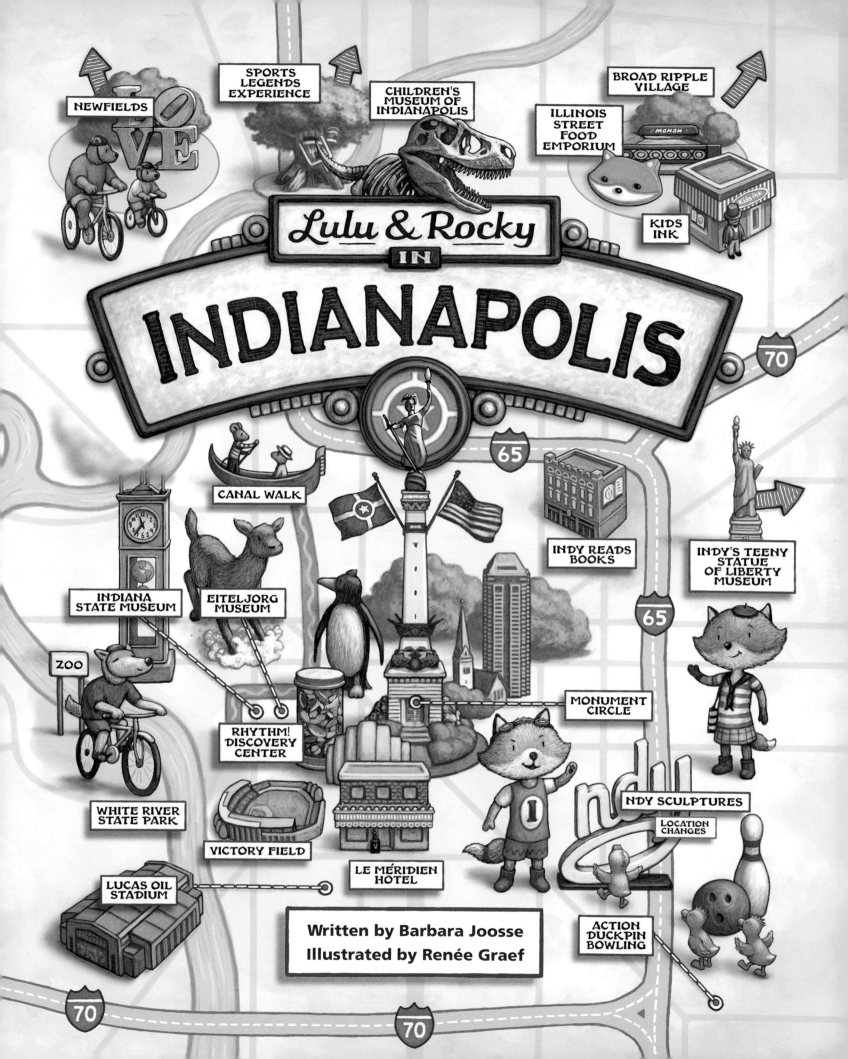

NEWFIELDS

SPORTS LEGENDS EXPERIENCE

CHILDREN'S MUSEUM OF INDIANAPOLIS

BROAD RIPPLE VILLAGE

ILLINOIS STREET FOOD EMPORIUM

KIDS INK

Lulu & Rocky
IN
INDIANAPOLIS

70

CANAL WALK

65

INDY READS BOOKS

INDY'S TEENY STATUE OF LIBERTY MUSEUM

INDIANA STATE MUSEUM

EITELJORG MUSEUM

ZOO

65

MONUMENT CIRCLE

RHYTHM! DISCOVERY CENTER

WHITE RIVER STATE PARK

NDY SCULPTURES

LOCATION CHANGES

VICTORY FIELD

LE MÉRIDIEN HOTEL

LUCAS OIL STADIUM

ACTION DUCKPIN BOWLING

Written by Barbara Joosse
Illustrated by Renée Graef

70

70

A purple envelope arrives.

Dear Lulu,

Are you and Pufferson ready for four days of adventure? Join Rocky and drive to Indianapolis in an Indy pace car! Then head to Le Méridien Hotel for your Adventure Assignments.

Aunt Fancy

Rocky's my cousin AND best friend. He gets his invitation by e-mail.

There's Rocky! We bear-hug and fox-box.
Pufferson checks his watch. He doesn't want to be late.

Then we pile into the souped-uppiest,
hot-roddiest car ever and drive past a building
with DINOSAURS crashing through the walls!

Holy Dinoly!!

"Welcome to Le Méridien and Hoosier Hospitality," says Mr. Johnny-Bear, the concierge. Then he winks and says, "Your aunt Fancy's right. You look more fun than a barrel of monkeys." Then he hands us our Adventure Assignments for today.

First up, the Children's Museum of Indianapolis.
We follow the crashing dinosaurs to Dinosphere.
When we hear roaring, Pufferson covers his ears.

"Don't worry, Pufferson—
the dinosaurs aren't real," Rocky says.

But I wonder. Are they?

Outside the museum is our next adventure—
Sports Legends.

We explore the Tree of Sports,
    and real coaches help us pitch, tackle,
        shoot baskets, and swing a racket.

SPORTS
LEGENDS

AVENUE OF
CHAMPIONS

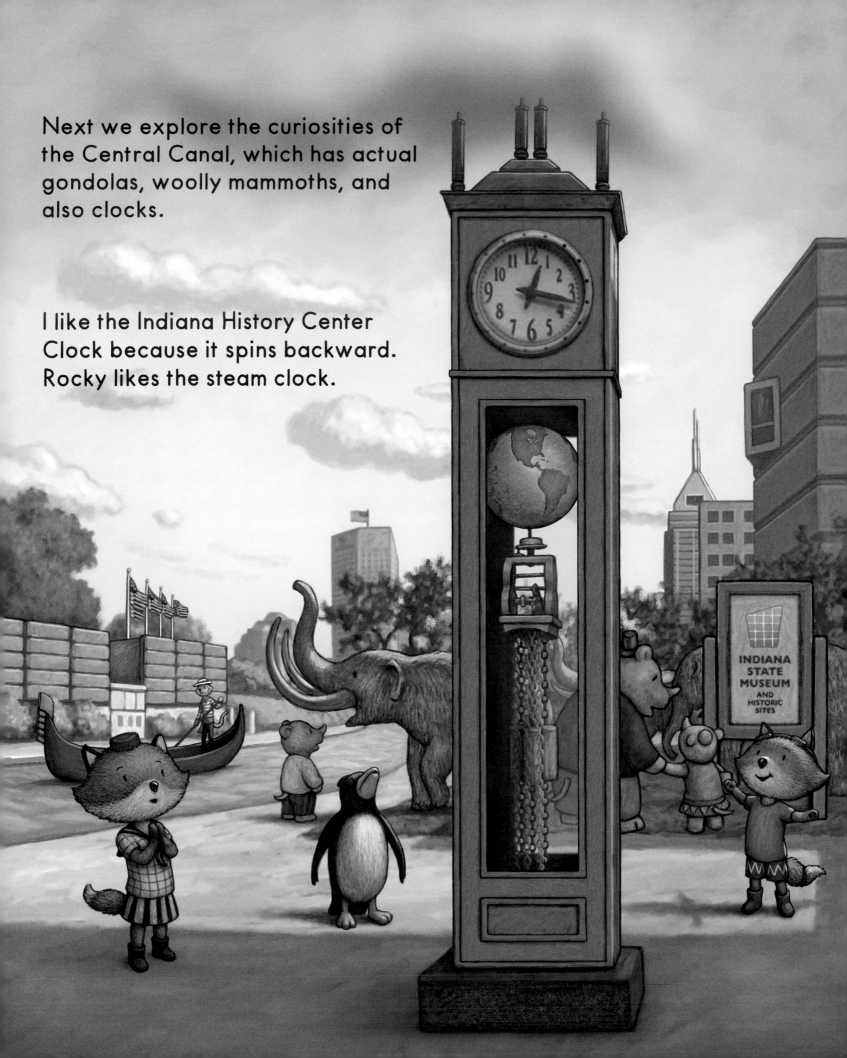

Next we explore the curiosities of the Central Canal, which has actual gondolas, woolly mammoths, and also clocks.

I like the Indiana History Center Clock because it spins backward. Rocky likes the steam clock.

INDIANA STATE MUSEUM AND HISTORIC SITES

We walk past "Big Blue," which is big and blue and reflects the puffy cloud Indiana sky.

Back in our room, Mr. Johnny-Bear delivers our Adventure Assignments for tomorrow along with mugs of steamy cocoa.

The next day, we start with the Eiteljorg Museum, where we learn about Western art by touching bison fur, doing puzzles, and drawing.

Then we ride a clip-clop stagecoach west
and text a picture to Aunt Fancy.

Next we head to Action Duckpin Bowl.
Rocky bowls a strike and does his signature
Rockarini Victory Dance.

In the afternoon, we pick up iced cookies that *look like us* at the Illinois Street Food Emporium . . .

and books that *feel like us* at Kids Ink.

Then we head to White River State Park.
We rent a surrey bike and hammock and pedal the park.

Then we chill with cookies and books.

In the morning, Mr. Johnny-Bear presents our Adventure Assignments in the Steve McQueen room. He talks into his hand, like a microphone: "Ladies and gentlemen, start your engines."

And we're off!

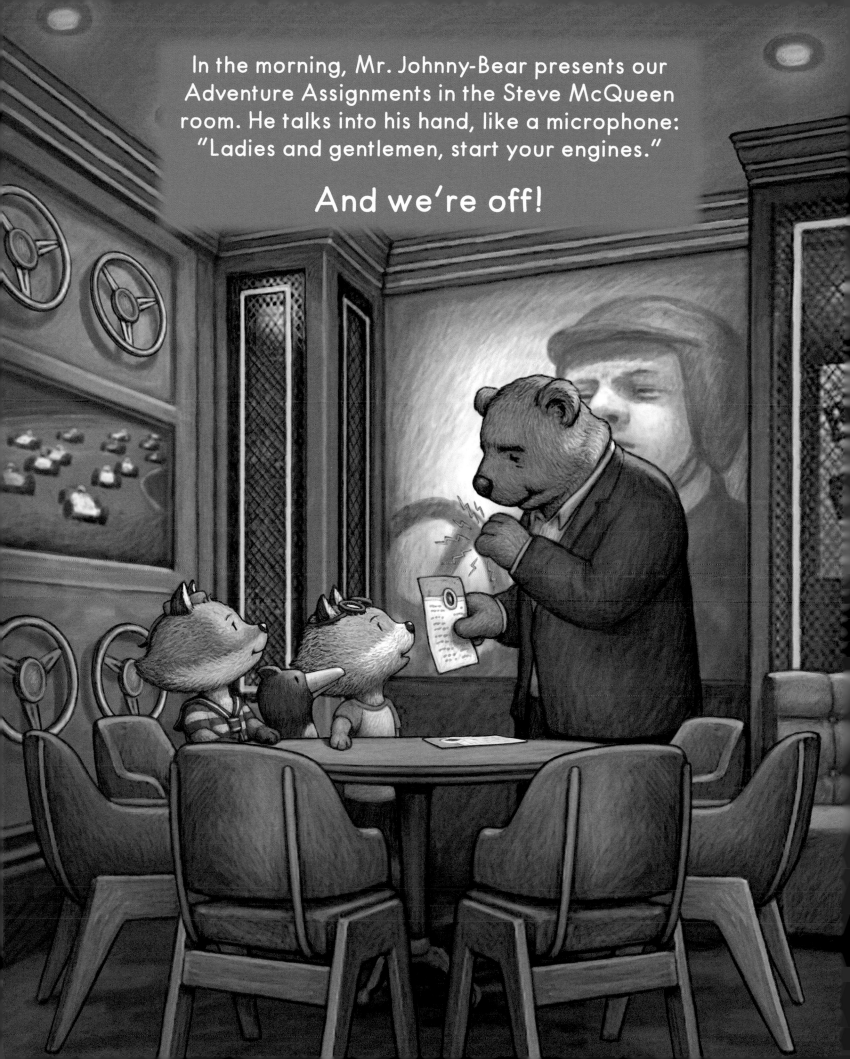

At Rhythm!, Rocky and I join a drum circle
while Pufferson gets happy feet.
Boom bucka
    Boom bucka
        Boom bucka
            BOOM!

At last, we head to the "brickyard"—
the Indianapolis Motor Speedway.

When we drive through the tunnel,
the actual track runs right over our heads.

Inside the museum, we examine Indy cars, racing suits, famous drivers, and trophies.

And I think, What would it feel like to drive that fast? What would it be like to WIN?

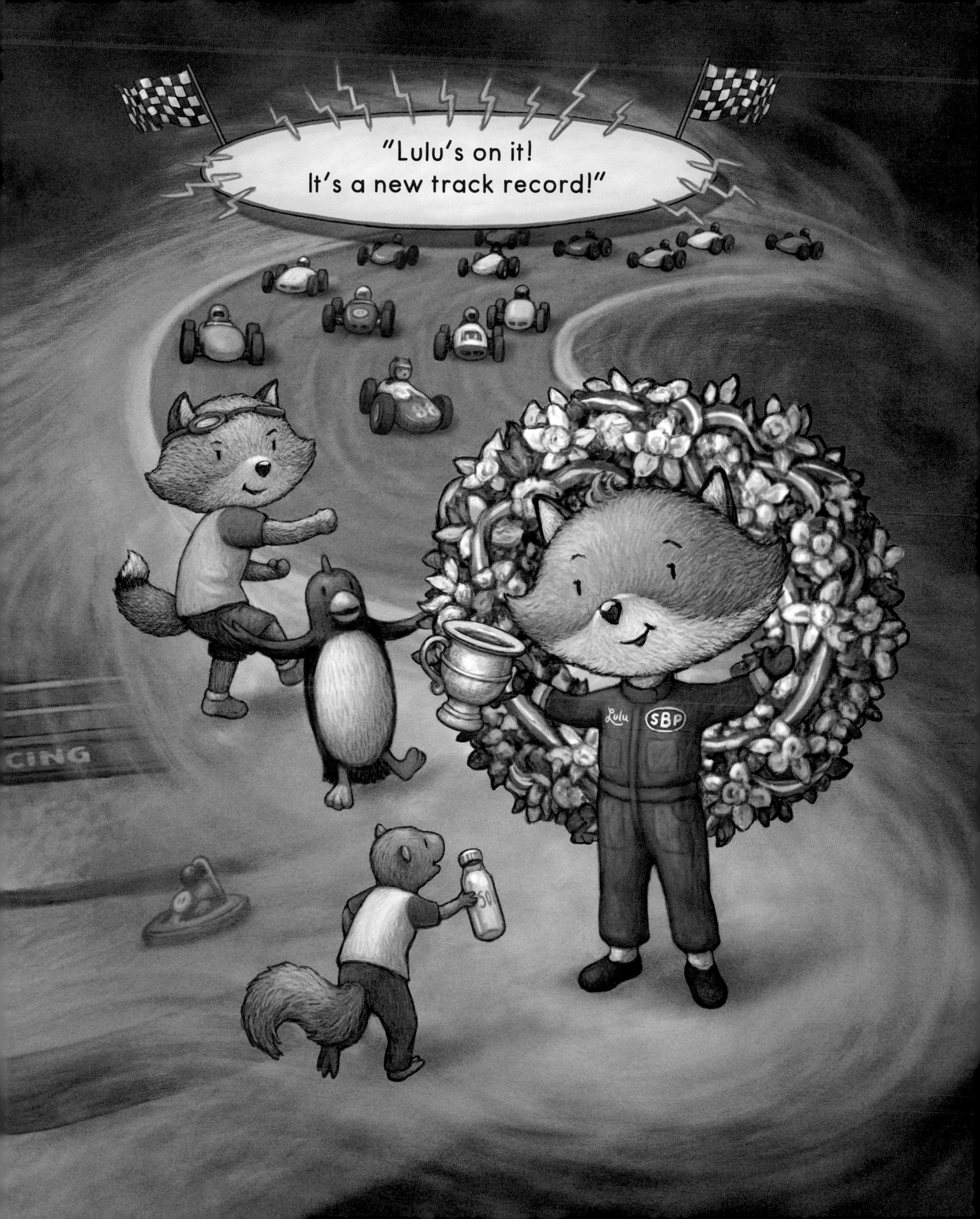
"Lulu's on it!
It's a new track record!"
Lulu
SBP

Back at the hotel, we paint our day.
Rocky paints cars,
Pufferson paints happy feet,
and I paint me, an Indy car legend.

On our last morning, we video chat with Aunt Fancy.
"THANK YOU!"

Then we say goodbye to Mr. Johnny-Bear.
"Come back soon," he says.

Then he scruffles our heads and gives us our last assignments.

At Newfields, we follow the twisty green path
to Funky Bones. We sing:

"Oh, the head bone's connected to the
spine bone . . .

and the spine bone's connected to the
hip bone . . ."

Then we go inside the art museum to LOVE.

Our very last stop is Monument Circle.
"Miss Victory" holds a golden light to
welcome us—and all!—with wide-open arms.

Now we don't feel like
visitors anymore.

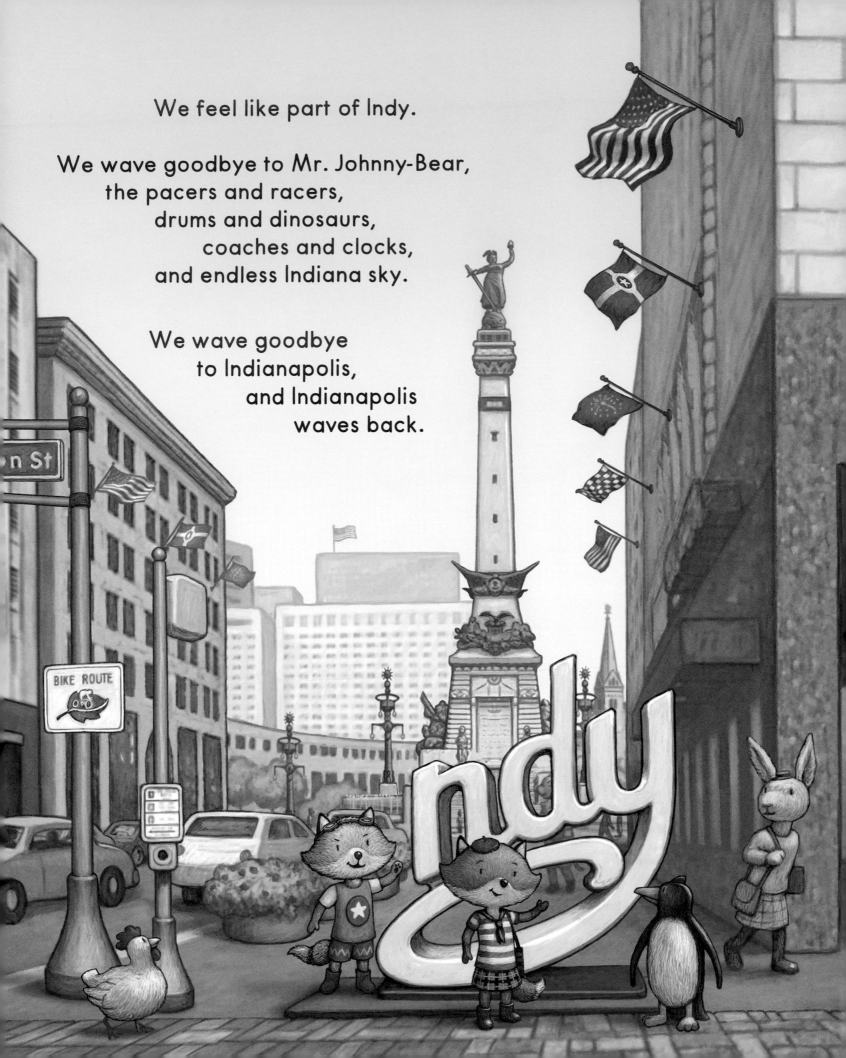

We feel like part of Indy.

We wave goodbye to Mr. Johnny-Bear,
the pacers and racers,
drums and dinosaurs,
coaches and clocks,
and endless Indiana sky.

We wave goodbye
to Indianapolis,
and Indianapolis
waves back.

MORE TO KNOW!

Indianapolis is a city with a wide-open sky . . . and a wide-open heart. You'll experience "Hoosier Hospitality" everywhere you go. Nicknames include: Indy, Circle City (because of Monument Circle), and the Crossroads of America (because it's the hub for several interstate highways).

Action Duckpin Bowl is a colorful 1930s-era alley, billiards, and café housed in the Fountain Square Theatre building. Duckpin bowling uses smaller balls and pins.

"Big Blue" is the nickname for the JW Marriott hotel because it's, well . . . big and blue!

At the **Central Canal** in **White River State Park** you can rent a gondola, pedal boat, or surrey bike, stroll along the art-filled promenade, and admire the Indiana History Center Clock that runs backward and the steam clock that releases clouds of steam—all in the heart of the city. And, if you get tired, you can rent a hammock!

The **Children's Museum of Indianapolis** is the largest children's museum in the world. At Dinosphere™, you walk in *their world* among exotic plants, rain showers, meteor showers, and roaring, towering dinosaurs!

Outside the museum, at **Sports Legends Experience**, you can climb the gigantic Tree of Sports and be coached in drills and skills by real coaches!

At the **Eiteljorg Museum of American Indians and Western Art**, you can snuggle up in a birch bark wigwam, toss buffalo chips on a fire, and ride a stagecoach. Don't forget to meet Wasgo the sea monster. Just tell him we sent you!

The **Illinois Street Food Emporium**, in Broad Ripple Village, has a family-friendly menu and is known for their iced cookies.

The legendary **Indianapolis Motor Speedway** is also called "the brickyard" because the entire 2.5-mile oval was once paved in bricks. Outside, you can take a lap on the Kiss the Bricks tour. Inside the museum, check out the cars, drivers, uniforms, and technology that became legends.

You'll find books galore at **Kids Ink**, a fabulous independent children's bookseller in Broad Ripple Village.

Le Méridien is a cozy boutique hotel in the heart of the shopping and dining district. Don't miss the Steven McQueen-Inspired Private Room! There's a secret door, but we're not telling you where it is. It's a secret.

Monument Circle is smack in the heart of Indy. The towering 284-foot, 6-inch monument was created to welcome soldiers returning from war. You can ride an old-fashioned elevator to the top to get a bird's-eye view of the city.

The popular **NDY** sculpture is the perfect place for a photo op. Just stand in the footprints to become the "I" in *INDY*. Created by Brian McCutcheon.

Newfields is the 152-acre campus of the **Indianapolis Museum of Art**. Outside, walk along twisty garden paths to Funky Bones, created by Atelier Van Lieshout, a Dutch art collective. Inside, you can see the famous LOVE sculpture by Robert Indiana. Mr. Indiana changed his name to honor his home state.

Catch the beat at **Rhythm! Discovery Center**. Try out hundreds of percussive instruments. Learn the drum pattern "paradiddle" and join the drum circle!

Speedway Indoor Karting is near—but not *at*—the Indianapolis Motor Speedway. You can experience live timing and scoring as you race around hairpin turns, yellow arrows, and a checkered flag.

Next time we're in Indianapolis we want to: see the Ice Age giants at the Indiana State Museum, shoot hoops in a 1930s retro gym at the NCAA Hall of Champions, and cheer for the Indianapolis Indians at Victory Field.